LOOK AND FIND®

MARVEL™
HEROES

S0-ARN-295

Illustrated by Art Mawhinney
Written by Caleb Burroughs

Published by Louis Weber, C.E.O.
Publications International, Ltd.
7373 North Cicero Avenue, Lincolnwood, Illinois 60712
Ground Floor, 59 Gloucester Place, London W1U 8JJ

Customer Service: 1-800-595-8484
or customer_service@pilbooks.com

www.pilbooks.com

Manufactured in China.

p i kids is a registered trademark of Publications International, Ltd.
Look and Find is a registered trademark of Publications International, Ltd.,
in the United States and in Canada.

8 7 6 5 4 3 2 1

ISBN-13: 978-1-4127-6665-4
ISBN-10: 1-4127-6665-6

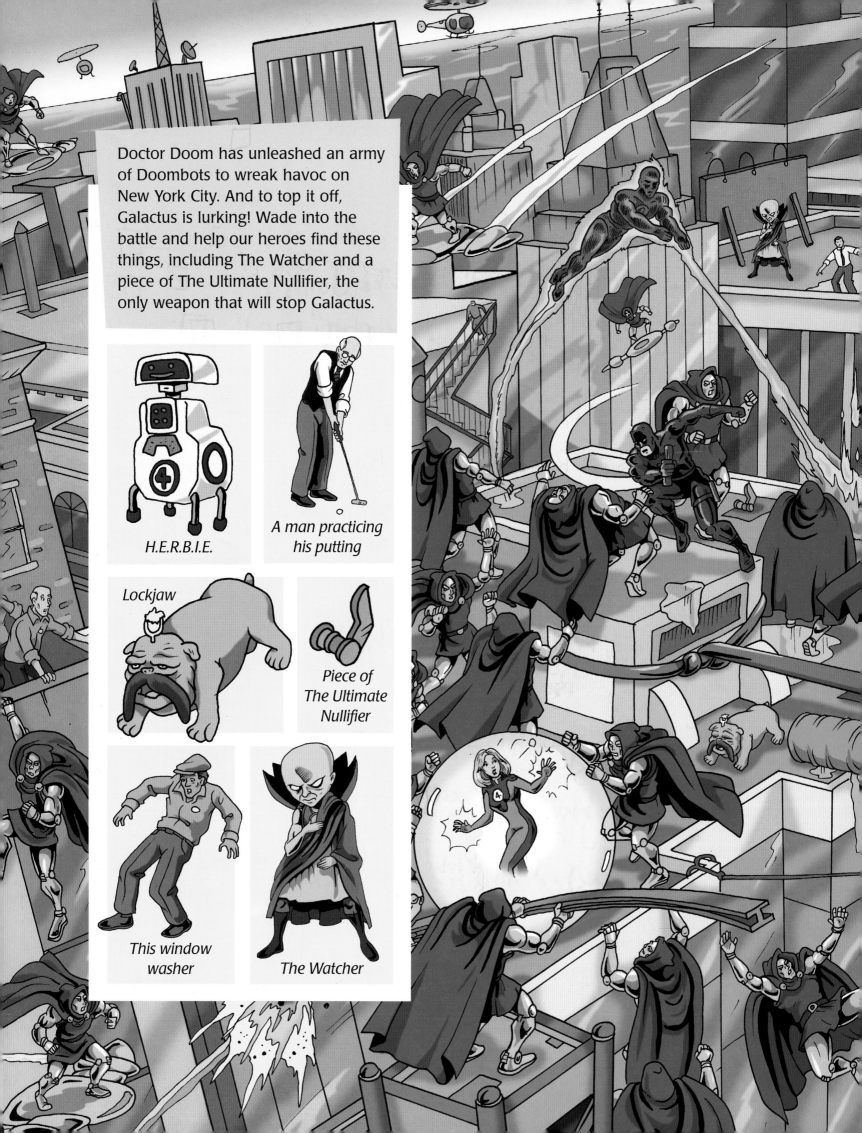

Doctor Doom has unleashed an army of Doombots to wreak havoc on New York City. And to top it off, Galactus is lurking! Wade into the battle and help our heroes find these things, including The Watcher and a piece of The Ultimate Nullifier, the only weapon that will stop Galactus.

H.E.R.B.I.E.

A man practicing his putting

Lockjaw

Piece of The Ultimate Nullifier

This window washer

The Watcher

Welcome to Professor X's Academy, where the mutants of the X-Men team hone their skills. Magneto and other enemies of our heroes have decided to attack. Look and find these mutant parts and pieces that will put a stop to the villains' onslaught.

Professor X's wheelchair

Archangel's wings

The Watcher

Piece of The Ultimate Nullifier

Wolverine's claws

Chunk of Iceman's ice

Cyclops's visor

Dr. Strange, Ghost Rider, Blade, and Wolverine find themselves battling a graveyard full of spooks and ghouls. Help our heroes spot these creepy creatures, then look for The Watcher and another piece of The Ultimate Nullifier.

This ghost

This zombie

The Watcher

This goblin

A vampire

Piece of The Ultimate Nullifier

In the big city, there are many workers who help keep things in order. But now these civil servants are in need of our heroes' aid. Can you find them, along with The Watcher and another piece of The Ultimate Nullifier?

Firefighter

Police officer

Street vendor

The Watcher

Piece of The Ultimate Nullifier

Letter carrier

This construction worker

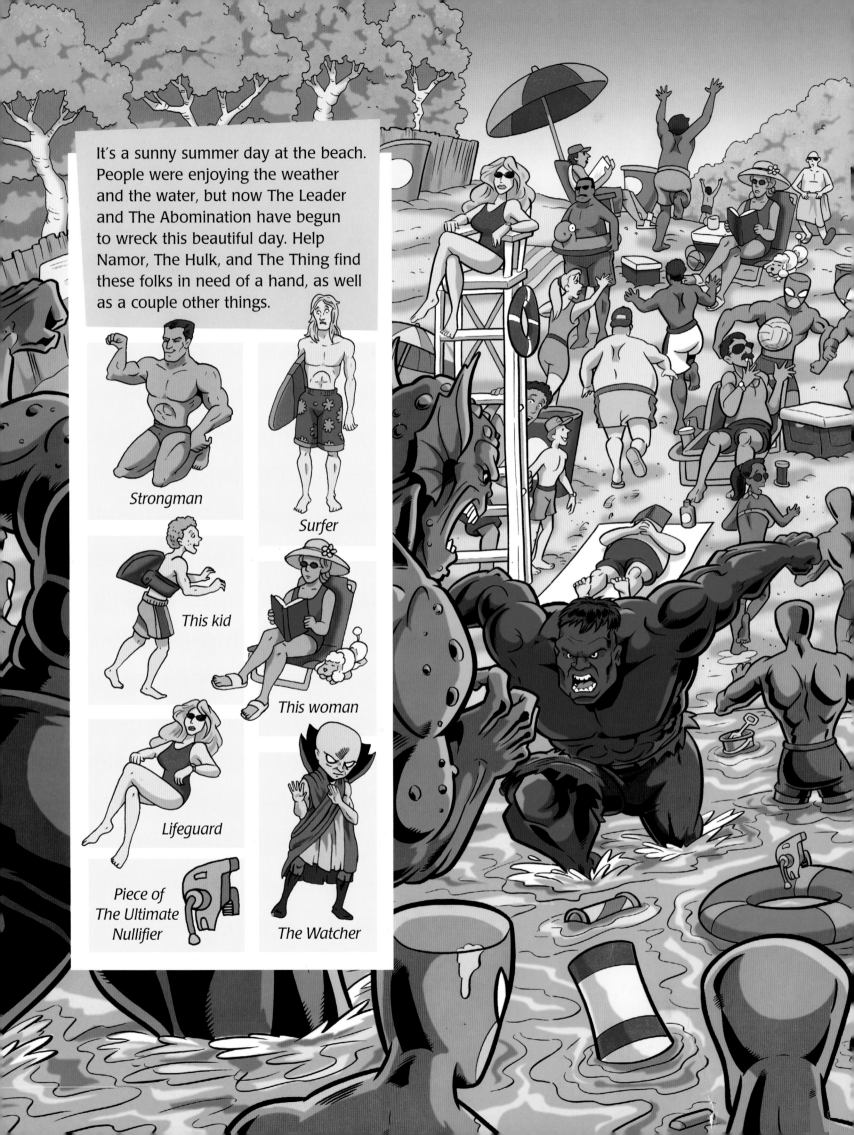

It's a sunny summer day at the beach. People were enjoying the weather and the water, but now The Leader and The Abomination have begun to wreck this beautiful day. Help Namor, The Hulk, and The Thing find these folks in need of a hand, as well as a couple other things.

Strongman

Surfer

This kid

This woman

Lifeguard

Piece of The Ultimate Nullifier

The Watcher

The Kingpin has decided to bring his criminal ways to this warehouse at the wharf. Only Daredevil and his friends can stop him. Sift through the action and spot these villains who might give our heroes a hard time. Then look for The Watcher and yet another piece of The Ultimate Nullifier.

Mickey the Mouth

Hairy Harrison

Franz Gruber

Piece of The Ultimate Nullifier

No-Neck Jones

Shady McShade

The Watcher

Wally Worrywart

DOCK 15B

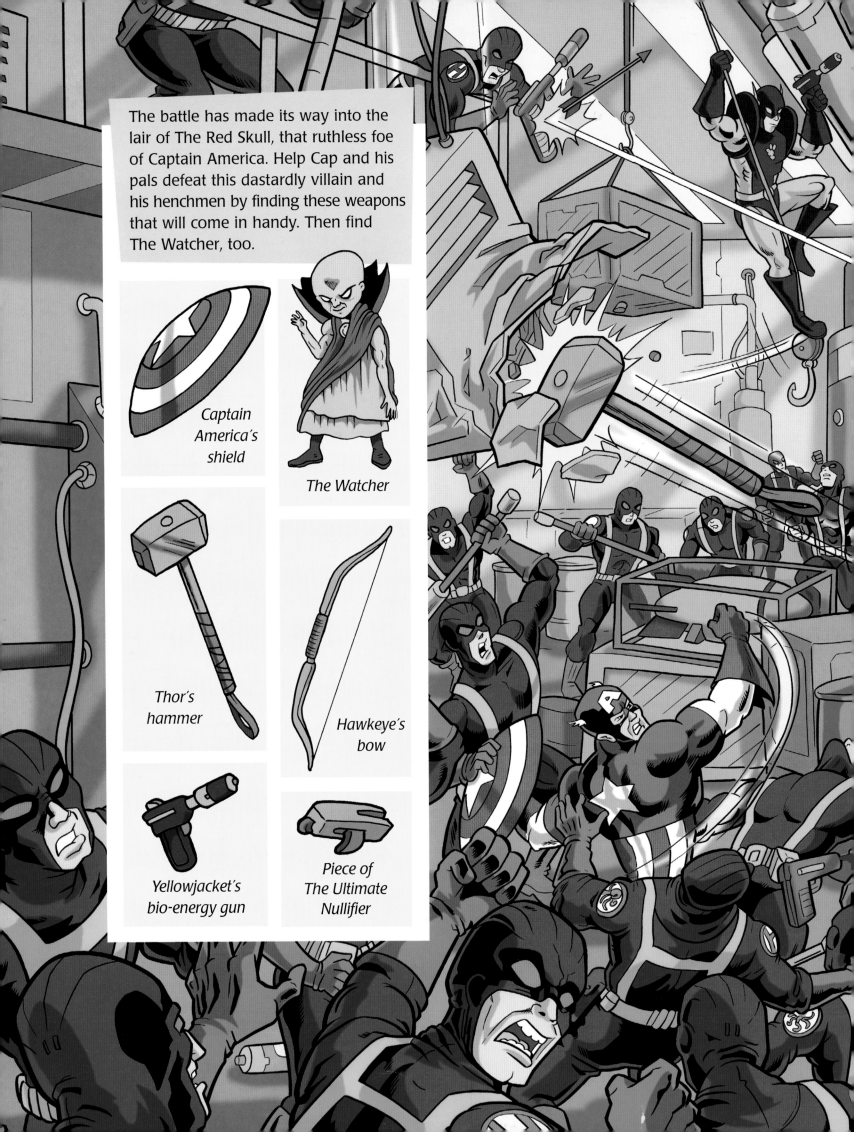

The battle has made its way into the lair of The Red Skull, that ruthless foe of Captain America. Help Cap and his pals defeat this dastardly villain and his henchmen by finding these weapons that will come in handy. Then find The Watcher, too.

Captain America's shield

The Watcher

Thor's hammer

Hawkeye's bow

Yellowjacket's bio-energy gun

Piece of The Ultimate Nullifier

Mr. Fantastic finally has The Ultimate Nullifier, the only thing that will stop Galactus. Find this important weapon, as well as these brave superheroes who are battling other evildoers.

Iron Man

Doctor Strange

Human Torch

The Ultimate Nullifier

The Watcher

The Punisher

Silver Surfer

Storm

Soar back to the rooftops of New York and find these defeated Doombots.

Head back to the Academy grounds and find these textbooks used to teach new mutant heroes.

Creep back to the graveyard and find these goofy, ghoulish tombstone markings.

Noah Moore Is no more	Daisy Pushing	Hamlet Good night sweet prince
This bloke went up in smoke	Silly Sally held her breath And now she's breathed her last	Sherry Cherry Choked on a chokecherry

Turn back to the city and find these traffic signs on the bustling and chaotic streets.

YIELD

NO PARKING BUS STOP

STOP

SLOW

BROADWAY

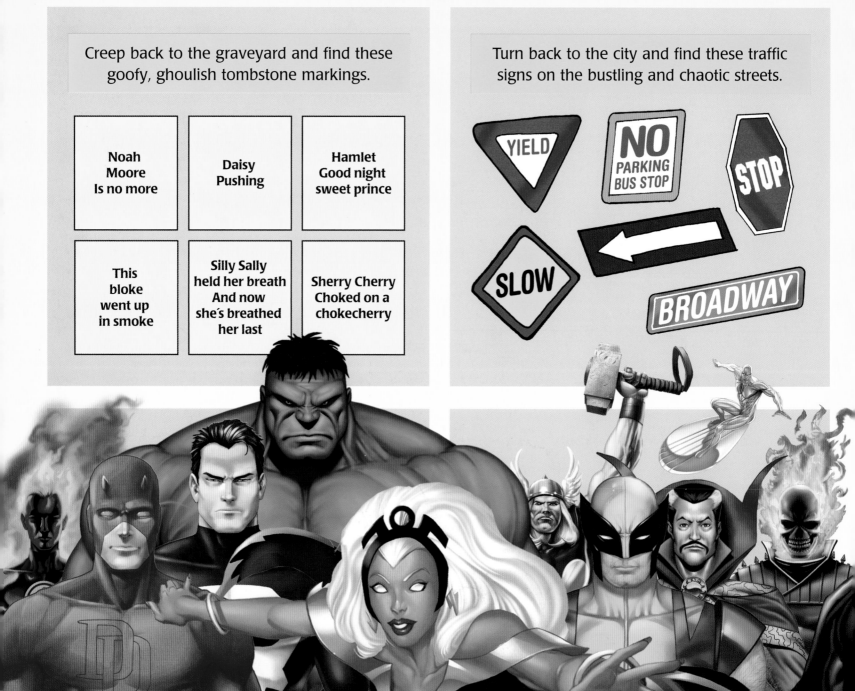

Boogie back to the beach to find this sandy, summer stuff.

Cruise back to the wharf and find these things in and around the warehouse.

Sneak back into The Red Skull's lair to find more weapons. This time, find these things that The Red Skull might use against our heroes.

Hurry back to the final battle scene and give our heroes a hand by spotting these six villainous ne'er-do-wells.

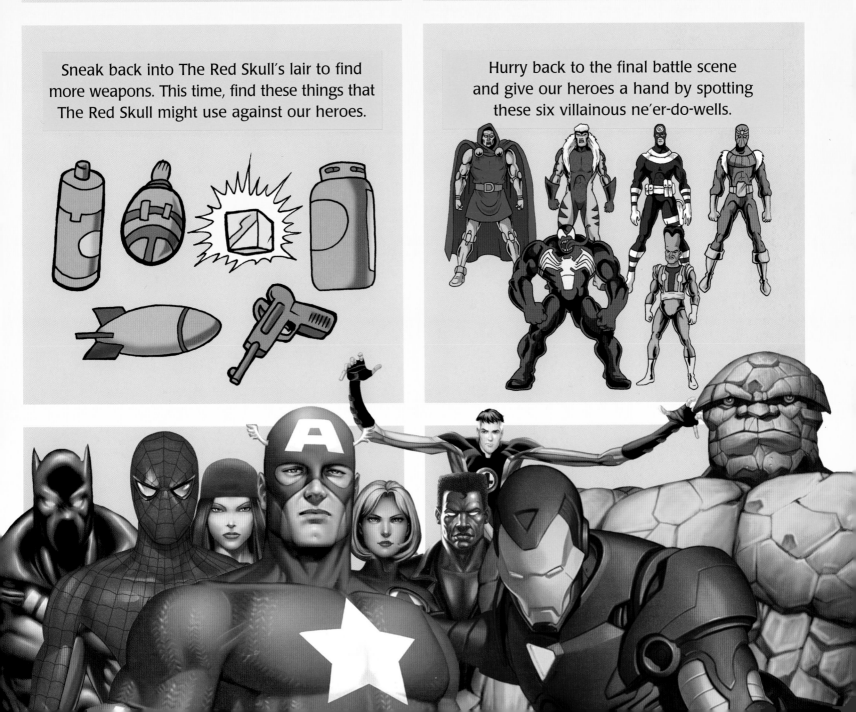